What If We Were All Kind!

C.M. Harris
Vitor Lopes

What If We Were All Kind!

Text & Illustrations Copyright © 2025 by C.M. Harris

Written by C.M. Harris
Illustrated by Vitor Lopes
Edited by Leila Boukarim

All rights reserved.

This is a work of fiction

No part of this publication may be used, reproduced, stored in a retrieval system, or transmitted in any form whatsoever or by any means, electronic, mechanical, photocopying, recording or otherwise, without the prior written permission from both the copyright owner and publisher.

Hardcover: ISBN: 978-1-63918-957-1
Paperback: ISBN: 978-1-63918-953-3
Paperback: ISBN: 978-1-63918-965-6 [Spanish]

Library of Congress Control Number: 2024926491
655 S Main St, Ste 200 #1130, Orange, CA 92868

Published by Purple Diamond Press, Inc 2025
This book can be purchased directly from the author.
Special discount for large quantities for schools/organizations.

Visit www.CMHarrisBooks.com for more information

Dedication

This book is dedicated to my niece and nephew. Always keep in mind to be kind, and may everyone you encounter, be kind to you.

~ Love, Auntie

WHAT IF WE WERE™ SERIES

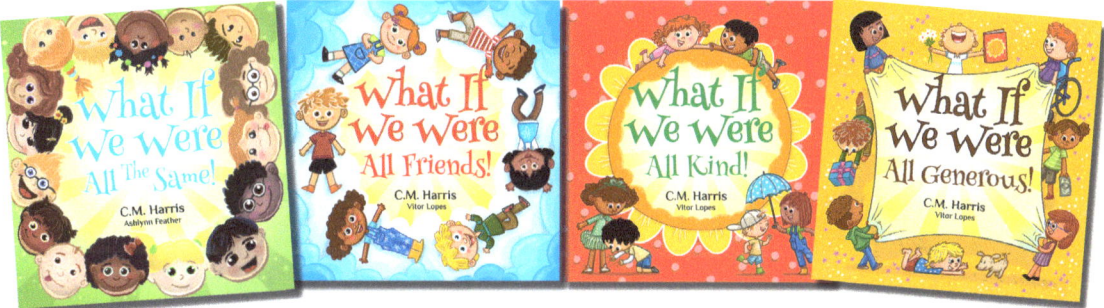

more coming soon

What if everyone chose to be kind?
A word to be kept on everyone's mind.

No more anger, no more fight,
just love and kindness, day and night.

No pushes, no tugs.
Just hugs! Hugs! Hugs!

Let's all show that we care,
and kindness will blossom everywhere.

We can travel near and far,
where we're accepted just as we are.

Helping a friend or someone new,
is something we really ought to do.

Kind words that are simple and sweet,
brighten the day for all who we meet.

Kindness at home and all through the day,
makes everything better in every way.

We share our toys, our time, our space, spreading joy all over the place.

One way to be kind: don't hit or kick.
We use gentle hands, that'll do the trick.

No screaming at your sister or brother.
Be calm! Then listen to one another.

When someone's sad or feeling down,
a kind word can erase a frown.

A little patience goes a long way,
so be very careful with how you play.

Take your time to understand,
be a good listener and don't demand.

Kindness comes in every size,
and as a team, we'll build and rise.

Helping hands and caring hearts,
community is where it starts.

We aren't all the same, so don't forget—
just be who you are, and you'll be set.

Please and thank you, you should say.
Let's practice kindness every day.

If you see someone sitting alone,
invite them over to your friend zone.

From friends to family and strangers too,
kindness is something we all can do.

Charity can be found in many,
let's all give, there's more than plenty.
Not just to people, but animals too.
They're just as important as me and you.

So you see, being kind isn't hard.
It's like planting love in your own backyard.

COMMUNITY GARDEN

If we all were kind, as kind as can be,
a world full of love is what we would see.

- - About The Author - -

Charity Michelle Harris, the award-winning author of **What If We Were All The Same!** and other great stories.

Charity lives in Southern California and enjoys visiting schools where she spreads the joy of friendship, acceptance, and inclusion. Charity loves working with children and was a private tutor for over ten years. She has her Bachelor of Fine Arts in graphic design, with a minor in marketing management from California Polytechnic University, Pomona. Charity is also the CEO of Purple Diamond Press, Inc. Born with a neuromuscular condition, Charcot-Marie Tooth Disease, Charity knows the joy of feeling included and accepted. What If We Were All Kind! is the third book in the What If We Were Series embracing kindness for people of all kinds.

To read more about Charity's journey, visit
www.CMHarrisBooks.com. Scan QR code.

I would love to hear from you, email me at **books@cmharrisbooks.com**

May you be so kind and leave a book review, every review is appreciated and helps very much.

Check out the other books

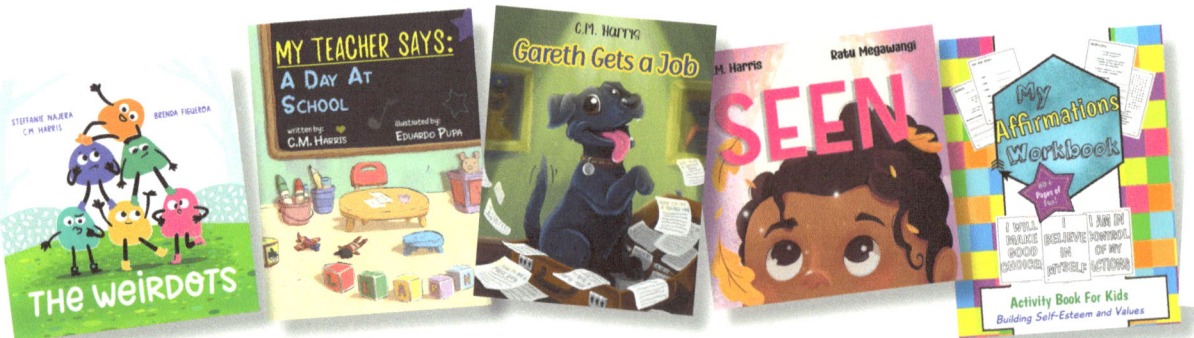

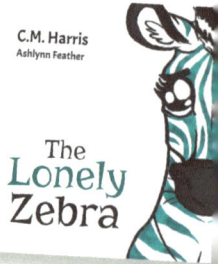

Discussion Questions

1. **What do you notice about the cover of the book?**
(Children can notice the differences of all the characters)

2. **What was your favorite page in the story?**
(Children can pick their favorite rhyme or point out what stood out the most to them)

3. **What are some ways you can be kind to others?**
(Allows brainstorming and highlighting individual qualities)

4. **How has someone been kind to you?**
(Allows reflection and appreciation of others)

5. **What does it mean to be a kind person?**
(Allows brainstorming and open conversation of genuine friendships)

6. **How does the story show that we all can be kind, even though we have differences?**
(Allows brainstorming and open conversation about diversity and inclusion)

7. **What did you learn while reading the story?**

About The Series

The What If We Were Series by C.M. Harris is a delightful collection of children's picture books that explores themes of acceptance, friendship, kindness, generosity, honesty, and more.

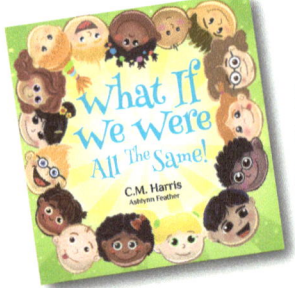

Discover the beauty of **diversity** in this inspiring story that teaches children to embrace what makes each person unique. Through vibrant illustrations and heartfelt rhymes, this book encourages kindness and acceptance of others.

Explore the magic of **friendship** as children learn the importance of helping, supporting, and understanding one another. This story highlights the value of forming connections and celebrating the bonds that unite us.

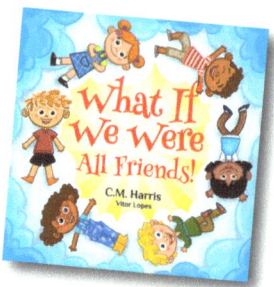

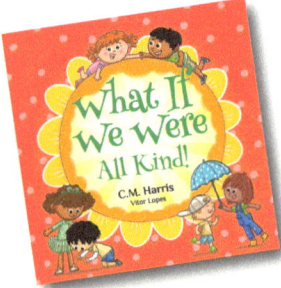

This uplifting book inspires young readers to spread **kindness** in their everyday lives through simple acts of care and compassion. With rhyming text and colorful imagery, it emphasizes the power of kindness to make a difference.

Teach children the joy of giving with this story that explores **generosity** in all its forms—time, kindness, and resources. Through relatable examples, kids learn how small acts of generosity can have a big impact.

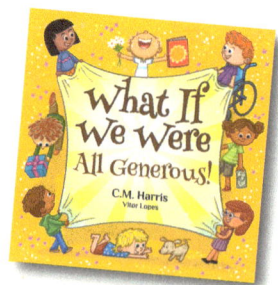

This thoughtful story encourages children to embrace **honesty** as a guiding value, showing the importance of truth in building trust and relationships. Through engaging rhymes, kids learn that being truthful is the best choice.

WANT TO MEET THE AUTHOR?

Invite C.M. Harris to your school or library for a memorable experience!

Ms. Charity loves traveling to read and speak to children of all ages. Ask your parent or teacher to scan the QR code to find out how I can come read to you!

Every visit comes with your choice of 2 readings and a fun presentation with a Q & A session with the author.

BILINGUAL EDITION

Discover the What If We Were series in a vibrant and engaging bilingual edition! Perfect for young readers and families, these beautifully illustrated books are now available in both English and Spanish, bridging language barriers and fostering cultural connections. Each story maintains its timeless themes of kindness, diversity, generosity, and honesty, helping children learn important values while developing bilingual literacy. Whether read at home, in the classroom, or during story-time, the bilingual editions provide an inclusive and educational experience for readers of all ages. Explore the joy of storytelling in two languages and inspire compassion across communities!

Check out the What If We Were™ Series!

www.ingramcontent.com/pod-product-compliance
Lightning Source LLC
Chambersburg PA
CBHW040943230225
22242CB00002B/7